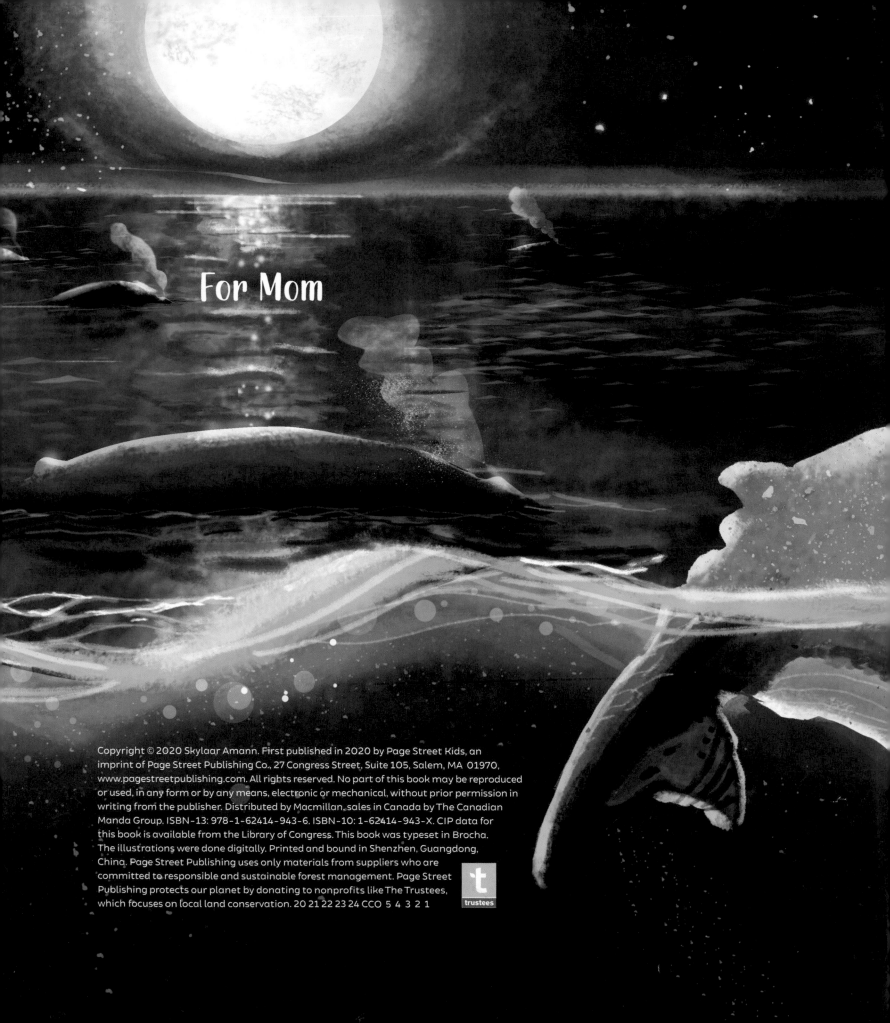

For Mom

Copyright © 2020 Skylaar Amann. First published in 2020 by Page Street Kids, an imprint of Page Street Publishing Co., 27 Congress Street, Suite 105, Salem, MA 01970, www.pagestreetpublishing.com. All rights reserved. No part of this book may be reproduced or used, in any form or by any means, electronic or mechanical, without prior permission in writing from the publisher. Distributed by Macmillan, sales in Canada by The Canadian Manda Group. ISBN-13: 978-1-62414-943-6. ISBN-10: 1-62414-943-X. CIP data for this book is available from the Library of Congress. This book was typeset in Brocha. The illustrations were done digitally. Printed and bound in Shenzhen, Guangdong, China. Page Street Publishing uses only materials from suppliers who are committed to responsible and sustainable forest management. Page Street Publishing protects our planet by donating to nonprofits like The Trustees, which focuses on local land conservation. 20 21 22 23 24 CCO 5 4 3 2 1

t
trustees

Lloyd Finds His Whalesong

Skylaar Amann

PAGE
STREET
KIDS

"Louder, Lloyd!" sang Mama Whale.
"If we can't hear your whalesong, you'll get lost!"

Lloyd visualized the whalesong.

"Aaaaoooo!" he sang.
But his voice was so quiet,
the other whales couldn't hear him.

The whalesong pulsed through the pod like a collective heartbeat. Each whale was like a star, and they formed a constellation that shone brightest when they worked and sang together.

This special melody kept the whales
fed, safe, and happy.

"The southern current is full of fish
and krill," trilled Grampa Whale,
and the pod ate their fill.

Its rhythm guided them through danger.

"Swim this way," sang Mama Whale.
"The water is warm and no harm will come to us."

The pod followed the whalesong to a quiet cove
to sleep for the night.

But Lloyd couldn't rest. He swam to the
nearby kelp forest. He felt at home in the silence there.

"Aaooo," he wept.
"How will I ever be part of the pod if I'm not
loud enough to join the whalesong?"

The kelp didn't answer.

Lloyd drifted through the kelp in silence
until his tail hit a strange object.

It had a long neck covered in symbols made of ancient, sea-tumbled glass.

Its body was carved from prehistoric driftwood.

And it had four storm-strong seaweed strings as old as the ocean itself.

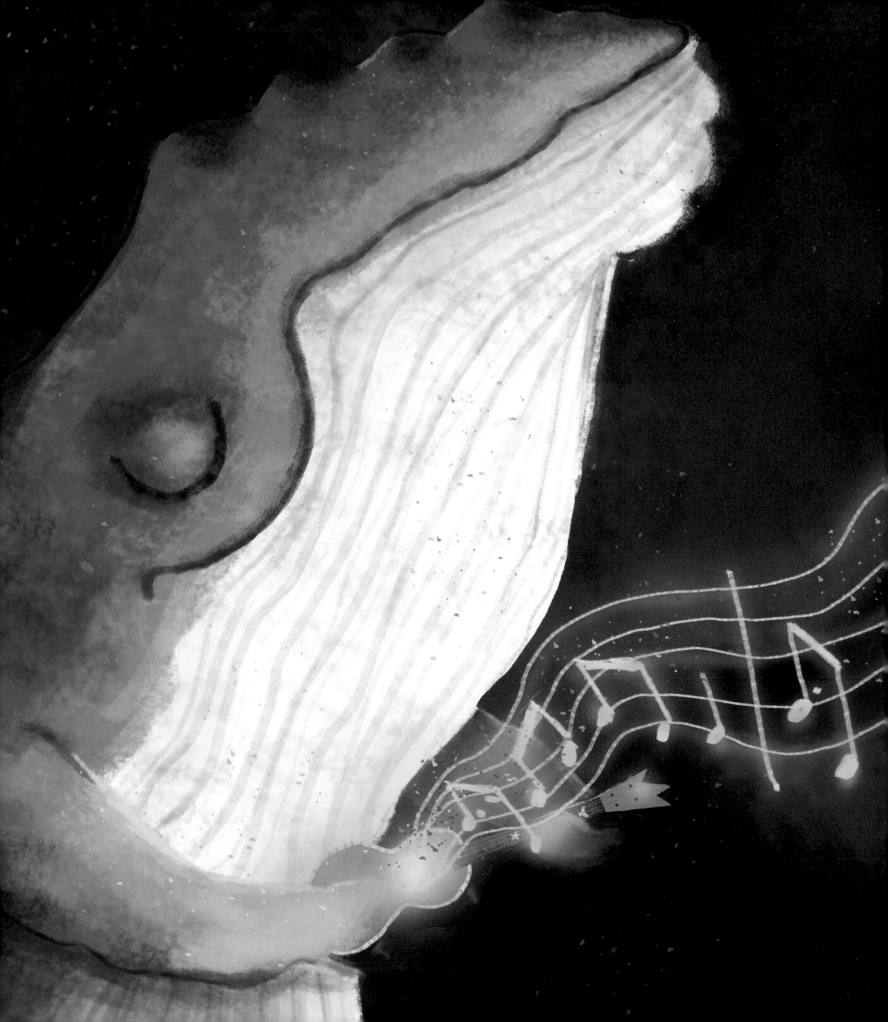

He tapped the strings, and they sang out:

Ba-ba-de-ba!

Lloyd gasped. He had an idea.

Lloyd hummed a few bars of the whalesong
in his quiet voice. He plucked out a matching melody.
Those little strings had a big sound.

Lloyd hid the strange thing in the kelp forest and returned every night to practice the whalesong.

And plucked.

He strummed.

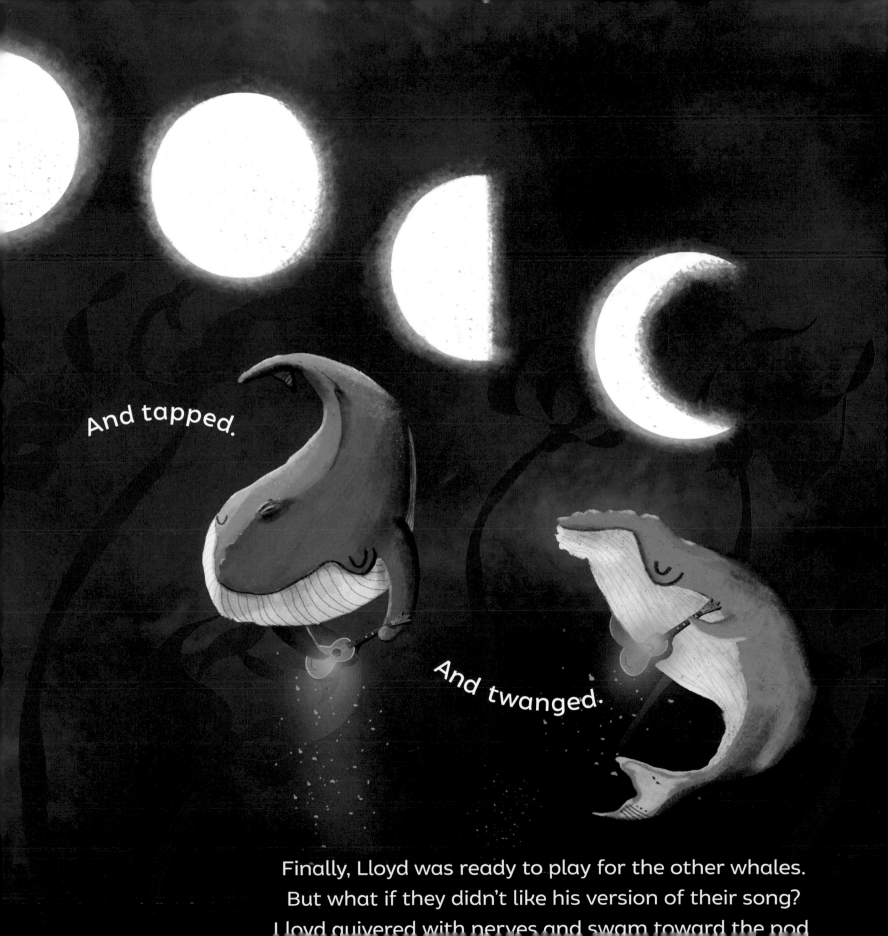

And tapped.

And twanged.

Finally, Lloyd was ready to play for the other whales.
But what if they didn't like his version of their song?
Lloyd quivered with nerves and swam toward the pod.

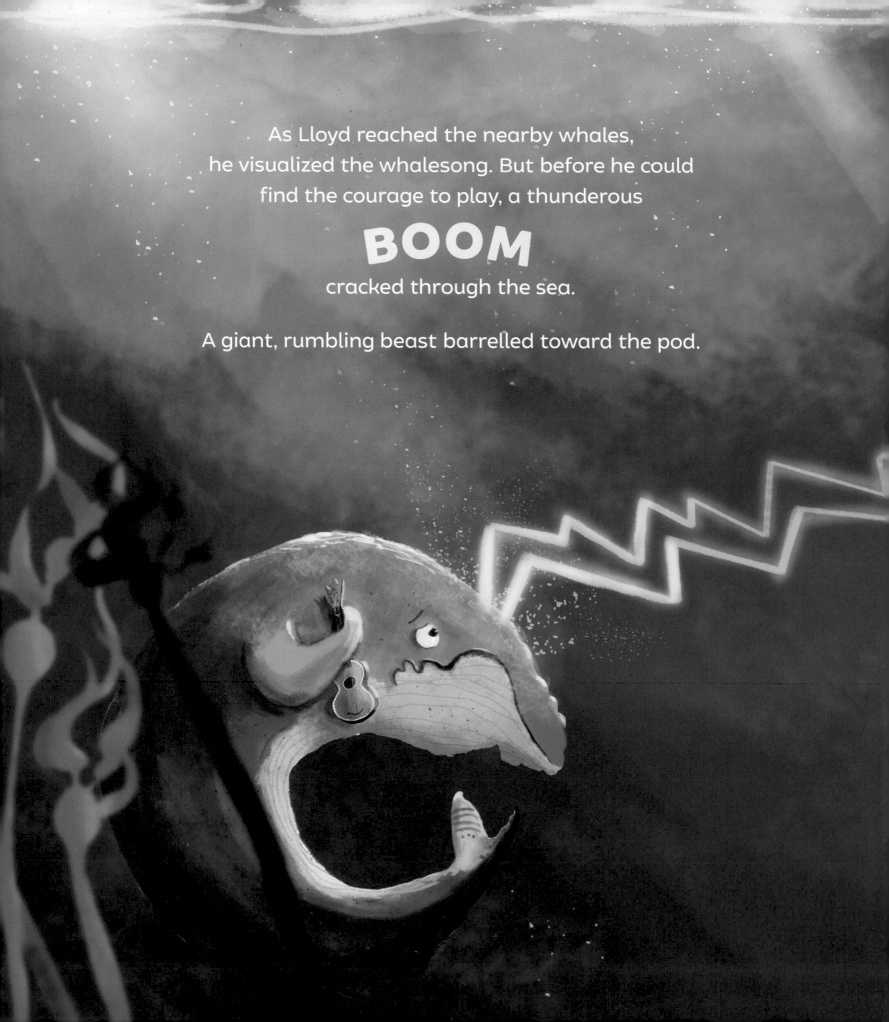

As Lloyd reached the nearby whales,
he visualized the whalesong. But before he could
find the courage to play, a thunderous

BOOM

cracked through the sea.

A giant, rumbling beast barrelled toward the pod.

The sound vibrated through Lloyd's bones.

The beast **HONKED.**

And **ROARED.**

And **RUMBLED.**

"SING!" Mama Whale bellowed as the rumble got louder. "Everyone sing loud and we'll stay together!"

The whales crooned in chorus, but the beast's roar drowned out their song.

"This way, Mama!" Lloyd squeaked, forgetting the instrument at his side. But the whales couldn't hear him.

Lloyd watched helplessly as the whales scattered.

"Mama?" Lloyd cried. But she didn't answer.
The whales, and their song, had disappeared.

But Lloyd realized he still had that little music-maker,
and he clutched it in his trembling fins. Would it work?
He visualized the whalesong and began to play.

Lloyd played the whalesong louder and louder
on that supersonic, wave-powered music-maker.

And the whales heard him.

In Lloyd's fins, their beloved whalesong reached across the loud sea to even the farthest-flung whales. The familiar rhythm swirled through the pod.

Their hearts pulsed as one, and they swam toward Lloyd and safety.

Lloyd played the final notes and
peeked up at the whales.

"Thanks to you and the way you played your music, we've found each other again," cried Grampa Whale.

Mama Whale smiled.
"What a beautiful whalesong you have!"

The joy in Lloyd's heart swirled like a wave hugging
the shore. He plucked out a grateful rhythm:
"Thank you very much!"

And with the help of that magical little
music-maker's big sound, everyone heard him.

Do Whales Really Sing?

The magical "whalesong" sung by Lloyd's pod, and adapted by Lloyd on ukulele, is based on a real-life phenomenon scientists call "vocalization" or "whale song." Humpback whales (*Megaptera novaeangliae*), like Lloyd, make long migrations across the ocean every year to breed, eat, and raise their young. They travel together in pods and use their song to communicate. Scientists don't fully understand whale song yet, but believe it is used for:

- Navigation as the sound bounces off objects and land masses
- Identification of other whales and predators
- Social interactions like breeding and sharing information

Humpbacks and other baleen whales sing by vibrating air through their vocal cords and special sacs in their throats. This mysterious singing uses a series of complex and repeating sounds, including pulses, clicks, and whistles. A whale's song can have up to thirty-four different sounds, remixed again and again over time through generations and pods. Humpback whales can sing for hours at a time, sending their sweet serenade up to one hundred miles across the sea.

The Dangers of Noise Pollution

The loudest sounds in the ocean are caused by human activity, including ship traffic, propeller noise, and military sonar. This noise pollution can disorient whales so much that they can become lost, veer off their migration course, lose their pod, or even strand themselves on beaches. Loud disruptions at sea can also lead the whales to become injured, starve, or even stop singing, which can reduce new births. Whales have even been known to die as a result of the noisy confusion.

Playing the Magical Little Music-Maker

Here is a short song loosely inspired by real humpback vocalization.

This song can even be played on a ukulele, Lloyd's instrument of choice!

"Lloyd's Song"

Thanks to ukulele teacher extraordinaire Marianne Brogan for her infinite wisdom.

Bibliography

McQuay, Bill, and Christopher Joyce. "It Took a Musician's Ear to Decode the Complex Song in Whale Calls." NPR. Last modified August 6, 2015. https://www.npr.org/2015/08/06/427851306/it-took-a-musicians-ear-to-decode-the-complex-song-in-whale-calls.

National Oceanic and Atmospheric Administration. "Soundcheck: Ocean Noise." Accessed March 12, 2019. https://www.noaa.gov/explainers/soundcheck-ocean-noise.

National Ocean Service. "Why Do Whales Make Sounds?" Accessed March 12, 2019. https://oceanservice.noaa.gov/facts/whalesounds.html.

Tsuji, Koki, Tomonari Akamatsu, Ryosuke Okamoto, Kyoichi Mori, Yoko Mitani, and Naoya Umeda. "Change in Singing Behavior of Humpback Whales Caused by Shipping Noise." *PLOS One* 13, no. 10 (October 2018): https://doi.org/10.1371/journal.pone.0204112.

Wu, Katherine J. "Ship Noises Mute the Songs of Humpback Whales." PBS. Last modified October 24, 2018. https://www.pbs.org/wgbh/nova/article/ships-noises-humpback-whale-song/.